Leigha was raised in a Christian family on a quiet farm in a small town. Over the years she fell in love with the nature all around her and found beauty in the smallest things. With an over-active imagination and a noted flair for the dramatics, she was encouraged to begin writing by her parents.

For Papa, who never got tired of listening to me talk.

Leigha Edwards

LOOKING DOWN

AUSTIN MACAULEY PUBLISHERS™

LONDON • CAMBRIDGE • NEW YORK • SHARJAH

Ordering Information
Quantity sales: Special discounts are available on quantity purchases by corporations, associations, and others. For details, contact the publisher at the address below.

Publisher's Cataloging-in-Publication data
Edwards, Leigha
Looking Down

ISBN 9781645758853 (Paperback)
ISBN 9781645362319 (Hardback)
ISBN 9781645758860 (ePub e-book)

Library of Congress Control Number: 2020924745

www.austinmacauley.com/us

First Published (2021)
Austin Macauley Publishers LLC
40 Wall Street, 33rd Floor, Suite 3302
New York, NY 10005
USA

mail-usa@austinmacauley.com
+1 (646) 5125767

God: Thank you for making this possible and for my family.

Mama: Thank you for being my biggest fan and my role model. You never questioned the people or the worlds I made up but taught me to be proud of the way I looked at the world.

Daddy: Thank you for teaching me to dream and always believing that I could do anything. You taught me to be strong and have the faith in my beliefs that I needed to make this dream a reality.

Ashley: Thank you for acting like I was crazy when I thought I couldn't make it. I couldn't ask for a better sister or best friend.

Mr. Michael Podurgal: Thank you for caring about your students. You are the only teacher I ever had who encouraged me to pursue writing and I wouldn't be here without you.

The Artist

It was supposed to be a white light, that's what they always say, right? "Go into the light," or whatever. I never saw any light, maybe it's different for everybody—I sure don't know—but I'm telling you there was no light. I can't remember much before I got here—memories of my life fuzzy and no recollection of the trip at all. But I know there wasn't any light. I'm sure of that. I was scared actually because it was so dark; then I heard this voice and believe me it was not what I was expecting to hear either.

"You going to waste eternity laying there?" the voice sounded oddly familiar, but I couldn't quite place it and I wasn't ready to open my eyes just yet anyway. I was still trying to become accustomed to the body I seemed to be inhabiting. It was familiar and foreign—mine and a stolen vessel—all at once.

"Mrs. Smith, that is no way to greet new souls." This voice wasn't familiar at all, but it was gentler than the first—calming in a way that proved only to grate on my nerves.

"Ms. Hannah," the voice called Mrs. Smith said—as though she was not particularly fond of the more friendly voice—guess that made two of us, "perhaps you would like to tend to one of the charges you have been assigned and let me handle mine in the way I see fit." Mrs. Smith did not seem well-suited to subtlety.

"No, that's okay, ma'am, mine isn't here just yet; I have plenty of time," I got the impression that 'Ms. Hannah' was only pretending not to hear the faint sneer in Mrs. Smith's tone. Almost made me like her a little actually. The surface I was stretched out on shifted as someone came closer and the younger woman spoke again. "Come on now dear, open your eyes for me." I'd have rolled them if they were open. Did she think I was a puppy? Did I get a biscuit if I listened?

"She won't respond to that." Mrs. Smith snapped, then suddenly something—I'm pretty sure a foot—nudged my shoulder. "Get up now, we haven't the time for this." The griping tone appealed to me more than the overly sugary one and I attempted to flex my fingers against my sides, trying to collect myself so I could do as she bid. My body remained still as I got no response from my extremities almost causing me to panic but the voices continued above me, unconcerned.

"You have eternity, Mrs. Smith." Ms. Hannah scolded her, "and you shouldn't kick them." The gentler feeling of someone dusting my shoulder off accompanies her words. I try to shy away from the unfamiliar hand—skin crawling at the touch—but don't feel myself moving; my muscles are completely unresponsive to my commands.

"Well, don't tell her that." I can't help but laugh at the exasperated huff and my eyes open as I do. Warmth floods me and my nose scrunches up as my fingers suddenly come back to life, digging hard into my hips from where I was still attempting to flex them. Above me stand two women, one smirks having won her argument and the other looks flustered by my sudden outburst. "There you go, she's awake. Scurry off." I recognize Mrs. Smith immediately and not just by the voice I've been listening to.

"I can stay if you'd like." Ms. Hannah, a younger woman offers but I just smile and shake my head. She frowns but reluctantly wishes me luck and leaves. I relax a bit as she takes her overly perky aura elsewhere.

I stare up at Mrs. Smith for a moment before taking stock of my surroundings. I'm lying flat on my back on some sort of soft, fluffy material. A little way away another body lays in a similar position only no one is hovering over them and I wonder how long I was here before anybody noticed.

"Well come along then," Mrs. Smith holds out her hand and I let her pull me to my feet. I expect the soft puff we're standing on to give way beneath my feet but it smooths out into a paved walkway and I follow behind Mrs. Smith easily, my body now working properly.

I feel like I should ask where we're going, or where we are even, but I can't seem to feel overly concerned. I trail behind Mrs. Smith at an easy pace and look around at everything. To our right, a group of children runs past laughing and screaming good-naturedly as they trip over themselves and each other. An elderly couple steps out of their way, the puffy, cloud-like ground hardening beneath them as their feet touch it. The woman smiles at them as their little feet patter on the walkway but there is a touch of sadness in her expression as she watches them, as well. I look the other way and see a pond sparkling in the bright sunlight. Behind that a honey-golden field of hay or wheat brushes over itself in soft waves as a gentle breeze ruffles the surface of the water. The banks of the small blue mass are littered here and there with men and women dipping lines in the water.

"So, all the choices in the world and that's what you choose to go eternity wearing?" Mrs. Smith's question guides my wondering eyes downward. I'm not wearing shoes but a fuzzy pair of socks, keeping me from feeling the strange ground.

Above that a pair of jagged jeans without knees, decorated with paint smears and splatters, hanging on by a thread to my hips. I'm wearing a white t-shirt that is also stained with half handprints and weird shapes left behind from a life-long habit of accidently leaning on wet canvases and paint trays. The piece of my outfit that gives me pause though is the thread-bare cobalt-blue hoodie tied around my waist.

I know Mrs. Smith is waiting for an answer but I can't focus on the question as my hands stray to the knot in the sleeves. I slip the worn cloth loose from itself, lift it off my hips, and pull it to my face with shaking fingers. The familiar, warm smell of Trey's cologne clings to the material and I feel tears burn the backs of my eyes as I crush the soft cotton against my face. I draw a ragged breath of his scent deep into my lungs before quickly tugging the jacket over my head when Mrs. Smith said my name in a much gentler tone.

"You're one to talk, of course." I say, finally responding to her question. She had to hear the choked catch of my voice but she decides to play along like I knew she would. Some things never change after all.

"Well at least I don't look like a hobo," she says, teasingly wrinkling her nose at my appearance. She tugs at the hem of her button up, smoothing the material over the tops of her slacks. "Now come along, we've got places to be," she turns away from me again and her sensible shoes continue clacking down our path. Fisting my hands into the too long sleeves so my fingers are tucked away I hurry after her. She stops without warning and steps off the path.

"Here," she says gesturing to the puff of ground in front of her as though I'm supposed to see something. She glances back at me and rolls her eyes at the confused look on my face. Looking around I see other souls kneeling and leaning or reaching into holes in the clouds. I look back at Mrs. Smith, still confused and step closer when she gestures impatiently at me.

"I don't understand," I say when I kneel next to her. I expect the clouds to be wet or cold but their comforting warmth seeps through my ragged, torn jeans.

"Well of course not, I haven't explained yet," she snarks, startling a laugh out of me and reminding me why she was always my favorite teacher. "When we get here the big guy...you know who I mean right?" she waits for me to nod before continuing, "Good, well when we get here the big guy decides—or already knows really—what we love the most. Teachers like me who love nothing more than guiding children and helping them are blessed to welcome newbies like you. We get to show them where they get to do what they love. Do you understand now?" she stares at me with the same expectant look she always gave me during class and I stare back blankly like I always did. Math was never my friend. The only conclusion I can draw from her words is that Ms. Hannah must be a kindergarten teacher or something. Have to have respect for someone who volunteers to be around that many small children but I still didn't think a conversation between the two of us would go smoothly.

"Not…really." I finally remember to tentatively tell Mrs. Smith, still wondering why we're kneeling on the ground.

"What do you love to do?" She prompts with a huff.

"Paint," I say without even having to think about it, a smile reflexively coming to my face, my fingers twitching for a brush I don't have. A brush I wish I had—I wasn't sure what I'd do if I did—but with paint in my hands the possibilities of what I can create are endless.

"Exactly," she says and hands me a smooth, polished wood palette and collection of smooth, soft looking, black wood handled brushes I hadn't seen sitting beside us. She brushes some fluffs of cloud out of the way to reveal a pile of jars of paint. I can't help the smile that curves my face and I reach for the colors but my fingers stop a few inches short as she gets to her feet.

"Are you leaving?" I can't help the nervous edge to my voice when I think of her leaving me alone. I don't really feel alone though—not because she's still there, or the other artists I can see working near us, no it's something else; something somehow deep inside me pressing in all around me at the same time.

"Not just yet." She says holding her hand out to me. I let her pull me to my feet again and she guides me over to the closest person to us. A girl who looks a few years older than me flashes us a grin and shows me what she's holding.

She finishes a few last-minute tweaks to a cat shaped mass of cloud cradled between her hands and as I watch she turns and tosses it into a hole in the ground. Stepping closer, I watch the cat grow as it falls, its legs move as though it's running and its tail flicks as it lands on a cloud and jumps to another. Finally, it settles on a low hanging cloud, kneads the material a bit beneath its feet the way cats do, and curls up to rest with a yawn and final flick of its tail. Farther down I see the Earth; unable to really see what's happening where I used to live, I let my eyes trace the sky instead. I watch the color burst and slowly flood along the horizon and look to see a boy with dark hair laying down to reach more easily into the hole in the strange ground in front of him. My chest thrums with excitement like my heart is beating too hard, too fast. He's painting the sky. It makes my fingers itch for a brush to see them creating this way.

"I want to try." I tell Mrs. Smith, who smiles knowingly at me. This time I lead her as I make my way back toward my jars of paint. I notice a hole has opened in the clouds next to them and kneel beside it. I look down at the sky— pale as a blank canvas—and the ground far beneath it, trying to decide what to paint. My eyes pass over the sleeves of the hoody I'm still wearing and I reach for the paint. I don't know whether to be surprised that there is a jar of the exact color or not so I decide not to worry about it.

I lean down into the sky and hesitantly draw the brush through the air. Color follows my motion on a much larger scale and my strokes become bolder as I decorate the sky, hoping Trey is looking up in the same place as I'm looking down. The eerie confederate blue darkens slowly to cerulean then further to cobalt. After a few minutes when indigo is starting to seep in as I shade the sky darker, I leverage myself out of the hole to show Mrs. Smith what I've done only to see she isn't there anymore. I look around but don't see her, instead I catch the eye of the dark-haired boy.

He smirks at me, raises a jar of bright crimson paint and bends down. I look to see my brilliant blue sky shaded over with red that quickly fades together into a deep purple. It doesn't smear like paint would but mixes perfectly. Smooth as marble, light shimmers over our canvas giving it an almost wet appearance and suddenly it's like looking into an eye, my breath catches. The window to the soul of the world. Grinning, I streak pink through our creation and he splashes orange over it all. Rather than shading into the purple, the pink floats in front of it a separate entity accenting the darker color. His orange settles delicately behind the other colors, a background of glowing warmth and a stark contrast to the deeper shades of blue. As we're working over each other, clouds suddenly come to life and crawl onto our work—slithering across like snakes in long, pale twisted lines. The colors we've strewn over the sky glow through the clouds and I know that somewhere far below, the three of us have created a beautiful sunset or sunrise—I can't really tell which from here but that's okay. It doesn't really matter.

I lay my paint brush down and settle my head on my arms. I can't quite see the buildings or streets on the ground from here but I can see the color-strewn sky. I can see the art work of the others here, scattered across it—my own painting now joining the mix.

I smile, content for now—just looking down.

The Musician

Silence. Darkness.

I scream but still no sound pierces the space I am in. Wherever that was, I thought back or tried to. My memory was as empty as this insentient purgatory.

Purgatory? Where had that thought come from? You only went to Purgatory if you were dead. I'm not dead. I can't be. I remember…-Nothing.

I don't remember anything. Well, I remember the nothing that I am currently inhabiting but even that, only a few moments of it.

I can't hear my heart beat; can't tell if my lungs are moving—what if they aren't? What if I am dead? I can't be dead! I have…I need to…I...

What do I have? I'm sure I left something behind at…at what? Did I have a home, a family, friends…anyone?
Even if I did, does it matter? All I have now are darkness and silence. Darkness and Silence.
Darkness. Silence.

Darkness. Silence.

Nothing.

"Can you hear me?" I'm not sure. Are you something?

"Open your eyes." Eyes? Those are definitely something. I think. They sound like a something. Sound is a something too. Why are all these somethings invading my nothing?

"Come on now, it's not so hard." Hard? Nothing is hard. But nothing is easy or nothing is soft. Hmm. It's also supposed to be quiet and this voice doesn't seem to get that.

"Just open your eyes already, kid." Kid? Someone used to call me that. It's not my name. I'm almost sure. Almost.

"It's rude to ignore people, you know?" The voice. I know that voice. It's…umm. It was right there, so close to remembering…something.

"You always were a stubborn one. I must admit I'd hoped you'd out-grown that particular trait." He mutters with a put-upon sigh.

My eyes fly open, my chest rising and falling rapidly, as I shoot up from where I'd been reclining on whatever it was. I stare at the man kneeling next to me with a wide grin on his face. Moisture gathered in my eyes as my lips tugged into a shaky smile. This is impossible, but that's okay. More than okay. So much more. I'd prayed to see this man who was the only father I'd ever known again every day since I lost him.

"Miss me?" Mr. Taylor asked.

Yes. So much, I thought as I threw myself at him; the understanding of how to move coming back to me without me even realizing it. Mr. Taylor was here. My memory had returned as well, I realized as he hugged me tightly to his chest. I remembered almost everything—not how I got here, but why I had to come.

I pulled myself back out of Mr. Taylor's arms to study the young-ish music teacher who had once showed me how to love life again. How to love anything. He'd taught me how to play piano and viola; made me see that not everyone was like my family; proved to me that life was more than fear and pain; introduced me to faith and showed me how to pray; and promised that he'd see me again, a smile on his lips and pain in his eyes the day that he died. There was none of that pain now but the smile was the same. The pain he had suffered as cancer poisoned his blood was washed away in this place just like he'd said it would be. Like I'd believed it would be.

"It's real," I whispered to him as I looked around. There was light everywhere but looking up I saw no sun. It was like the light was just inside of everything and spilling out to brighten the air itself. I could smell water in the distance—a lake or pond—but closer than that I smelled vanilla and cinnamon like someone was baking nearby.

"You knew it was," he says back, smiling when I look at him with wide, confused eyes. "You knew it was," he repeats, "or you wouldn't be sitting here."

He gets to his feet and I can't help but smile at his easy movements—gone is the pained stiffness he could never hide as well as he thought. He offers his hand and pulls me easily to my feet. He turns his hand when I stand beside him and holds it up so our palms face each other. Despite being nearly a foot shorter than him, my slim fingers were long enough to reach the knuckle nearest his fingertips.

"A musician's hands." He murmured the same words he'd given me the day we'd met; I'd rolled my eyes and snatched my hand away. Today I smiled.

Dropping his hand from mine he turned and started walking down a thin path correctly assuming that I'd follow him. We walked in silence for a while as I tried to take everything in. The air was warm, filling my lungs comfortably as I drew in a deep breath. We passed by a group of people ranging from, around my age of 15 to well older than Mr. Taylor. They laughed as they knelt in the clouds throwing what might be paint into holes I can't really see from where we're walking. Weird.

"Artists," Mr. Taylor announced, without looking back at me. I frowned at the back of his head, and he turns to look back at me as if he could feel my stare. "That's what we do here, Nika. Whatever we always loved most. He gave us gifts so we could honor Him on Earth and now He rewards us by letting us continue our passion here." He continued walking then, slowing so we were side-by-side instead of me trailing along behind his longer stride.

"What's your passion, Mr. Taylor?" I questioned, curiously. I assumed music like me. Maybe that was why he came to get me from the field I had woken up in—to show me where he played his music. So we could play together.

"Teaching," he said. I looked at him in surprise. How could anyone create music the way he always had without it being their passion? Seeing my look, he continued, "I love music, yes, but I love helping people who need me more." The way he had helped me when I thought I was beyond saving.

We finally came to the water I'd been smelling and I frowned at the river in front of me. It wasn't huge, more of a creek really with muddy banks decorated by sparse grass and tall water-reeds. It was beautiful as the same light that encompassed everything else danced over the ripples where rocks cut through the surface of the water. The reeds stood tall without any wind to blow them, sentries along the water's edge as though waiting for a threat or miracle to come and free them from their muddy station. It was beautiful, but unsettling. It was quiet. Too quiet. Silent. The river that should have hissed and sighed as it brushed over rocks or gurgled and chugged as it was once again gulped into itself when it fell from splashing up to keep the bank from drying out didn't vocalize its existence in the slightest. It was silent. It was wrong.

"Why is it like that?" I ask, after waiting as long as I could stand for the river to express itself in some way; to tell my ears, not just my eyes that it really was there in front of me. To let me know in the way closest to my heart that it was real.

"It's waiting for you." Mr. Taylor says simply. I wait for him to continue but he has fallen as silent as the eerie river he stood watching calmly.

"What?" I finally asked, in all my eloquence. He laughed loudly before turning to face me.

"An instrument doesn't play without its musician, does it Nika?" He collected himself into the role of teacher easily, looking comfortable in the part.

"No," I answered hesitantly. What does that have to do with a creepy, silent river?

"Then you have your answer," he said seriously. He must have lost it. That makes sense. He's just crazy. I let him know about these thoughts with the look I favored him and he laughed again, not offering up any argument to defend his sanity.

"You're telling me to play a river?" he nods. "A river is not an instrument, Mr. Taylor." I speak slowly, trying to make him understand how crazy he sounds.

21

"Are you sure?" I start to nod, but hesitate. Am I? How could I be, really? This place isn't like anything I know so how can I be sure you can't play a river. "Exactly," Mr. Taylor says, like he can read my mind. Maybe he can or at least my face; he certainly knows me well enough for that. "Try it."

Try it. Okay let me just do that. Try it. Pfft. Try what exactly? How does a person play a river? He's obviously not going to tell me that. I'll just have to *try it*. Rolling my eyes, I make my way toward the river, stomping just a little to let him know I am unpleased. He makes no comment but laughs when I slip in some mud. I barely manage to stay on my feet and don't give him the satisfaction of turning to glare at him. Unsure what to do now that I'm right on the edge of the river, I let my hand trail over a few water reeds that stretch up around my hips as I stand among their guard, jumping when sound suddenly tears the silence open.

A low thrum—that of a plucked cello—fills the air for the briefest moment and I spin around to stare at Mr. Taylor. He looks further away now but he grins when he sees the excited wonder on my face. I turn again to the reeds and more deliberately brush my hands against them. Each one makes a slightly different tone but all have the deep resonance of cello that steals your breath and settles in your bones in the most exhilarating way. I strum them faster until their tempo matches the beat of my heart.

I move then to some of the lower reeds, flicking my fingers over them to hear the higher sound of a violin. Perfectly tuned notes dance as I brush my fingers over the heads of the reads. I played them for a while before standing to move on again, only I slipped in the mud. My hand fell then into the water as I struggled for balance. It made a sound like none I'd ever heard before. It sank into me and I couldn't help doing it again and again. It wasn't like any instrument I'd heard in my life—almost too perfect to call both sounds by the same name. I stepped into the river to get access to more water but I didn't sink like I had expected to. Giggling, I ran and danced over the water, happier than I ever remembered being.

When I reach the middle, I found a large rock sitting an inch or two beneath the surface. I sank to my knees and as I settled over the rock, the water finally embraced me. When my knees touched the surface of the rock, it began to thump with a deep, base sound in the rhythm of my heart beat. I settled my fingers over the water as though playing a piano and began to stroke over the ripples like shiny, ivory keys. That same aweing sound rose around me and I laughed out loud in pure joy harmonizing with the soul-filling thrum of the river.

As I played a sound came through my mind. I wasn't exactly hearing it; it was more like it was being put directly into my mind without traveling through my ears. It was the sound made by a river like this on Earth. I continued to play as I listened and soon realized the Earthly river was echoing the sounds I made here. Heart in my throat, at this revelation I raised my eyes to Mr. Taylor but he wasn't there. I looked all around but he wasn't at my river anymore. I was alone.

My fingers fell still. Both songs playing in and around me stopped as well. Alone, I knew the feeling well but I had been so happy here that I let myself hope not to feel it again.

I was beginning to doubt how wonderful this place actually was when a sound reached my ears. A different sound than my river made. Someone downstream was playing the river as well. I listened as they played an elegant song, smiling to myself as I added some deeper tones to their piece. Their song cut off abruptly and I was worried I'd offended them but then the sound came again. It was short, sharp and high pitched—somewhat like a flute or piccolo—but like the other sounds, it was too clear and honest to really be the same. The same set of notes came again, a moment after they'd cut off sounding almost challenging. The third time they rang through to me, I echoed them back at lower resonance. A new set of notes answered immediately and I grinned as I picked up the dog-fight.

Back and forth, we kept changing key and tempo like we'd been playing together on these strange instruments for years rather than moments. Playing together, I smiled again. Maybe I wasn't alone. I had music and people to play it with; people who loved and understood music like I did.

No, I wasn't alone at all.

I was home.

The Dancer

I could hear music; could feel the way it thrummed deep in my bones; could feel my muscles tensing in preparation to move—but I didn't know the steps; didn't know the song; didn't know what stage I was on or what part I was intended to play on it; didn't know why it was so dark.

The music changed and took on a quickening tempo. It was racing toward something and I wanted to join it. I was desperate to know what it was after, hoping that there was something—anything—in this place. Along with the tempo, the volume rose and drug my heart along with it. We reached the peak of the crescendo and a blinding light—like staring straight into a spot light—filled my vision. I blinked against the burn of the light and it slowly faded back, allowing my eyes to focus on what was happening around me.

To one side a couple spun, the man lifting the woman into the air before supporting her as she bent backward till her shoulder length hair brushed the floor before tugging her up to spin under his arm. The woman's silky skirt twirled around her as she twisted and spun on her toes. The man watched her with love-struck eyes as he shaped her movements. Both dancers smiled as they moved, the looks softening to something intimate and personal whenever their eyes met. They moved together perfectly; he led but she was in control. He might choose what moves they made and when but every move he dictated was aimed to bring her joy. When he lifted her, she laughed with the unfiltered pleasure of a child; he dipped her and she looked up at him like he was the only thing in her life that mattered; he spun her out and she returned as though being separate from him was painful to her. He touched her like she was spun from silver—careful like he knew she could break if stretched too thin but not in a way that could be called delicate, trusting her to be strong enough to meet the challenges he offered her.

Off to the right of them, a girl danced by herself. She spun and twisted, impossibly graceful and poised on her point-shoes. The starched tulle of her tutu standing out bright pink against the pale clouds behind her.

Wait. Clouds? What?

"Beautiful, aren't they?" My head jerks around to find a small woman sitting cross-legged beside me. Her hair is pulled into that perfect bun that I've never understood how ballerinas manage. I mean honestly, all the spinning they do their hair should not stay that…that—I don't know—*round*. I just don't get it. Girl-thing, I guess.

"Um…" my wonderfully articulate response gets a raised eyebrow. What can I say, I'm better at getting a point across with motion than I've ever been with words.

"The flowers," she says, rolling her eyes and pointing when I just looked confused. "Look."

Back behind the girl in pink there is a large mirror, the kind you see in every dance studio with a barre in front of it. They let you watch yourself so you can critique yourself when no one else has the time. This one isn't reflecting though. Instead, it shows a field of overgrown grass and pink wildflowers. There is no sense in where the flowers spring up throughout the large field—not until I look at the girl again. Her elegant dance is reflected in the mirror after all. Every place her foot lands between leaps and twirls, a flower crops up in the field. She spins, quick and repeatedly on one foot, and the flower grows into a bush with multiple blooms proudly reaching toward the sky.

I look to the couple again, still awed by their perfectly synchronized grace, then I move my gaze past them to the large studio mirror I hadn't noticed before. There are no flowers here but rather a large maple tree blushing in the autumn cold as leaves dive and sink from their high perch. I follow the decent of two leaves as they fall to the ground. One is a furious red and the other an equally vibrant orange—they stay close together, intertwining and brushing against each other as they drift in a nonexistent breeze. They are following the pattern of the couple dancing in front of me. He is the red, she is the orange, and they move as weightlessly as the leaves they are reflected in. When those leaves touch to the ground, they don't stop and another set of leaves loose themselves from their branch. They come together – a bright yellow led by a faded green, picking up the choreography without a hitch. Widening my focus to look at the whole mirror, I see a child running and jumping beneath the tree; grinning ear-to-ear as she tries to catch the falling leaves before they hit the ground. Her laughter mixes with the music flowing through the air to create the most beautiful sound.

"Yea," I murmured finally, "They're amazing." Her chuckle is quiet as my eyes stay locked on the dancers' motions.

"You like to dance, right, Luke?" Her question is enough to draw my attention to her.

"How do you know my name?" I ask her, unable to keep the accusatory tone from my voice but she just laughs again.

"He told me your name when He asked me to show you the ropes." Well that really just opens more questions than it answers.

"Who told you? Where are we? What do I need to be shown?" I scoot a little further away from her and she laughs at me.

"Thinks about it, Luke. Think about the last thing you remember before you woke up here." I close my eyes and try to do as she says. The memory comes readily to mind and I quickly open my eyes to stop seeing the graphic scene.

"I'm dead," I say. It's not really a question but I need her to tell me it's true all the same.

"Yea, you are." I knew I was but I still flinch when she says it so matter-of-factly. "So, you know where you are then. You'd have to if you got here." Another little laugh. I give an absent nod, too busy trying to come to terms with being dead to care about what she's saying. My eyes stray back to the dancers and I relax as I watch them move. "Now back to my question, you like dancing, yes?"

"Yes," I say without looking at her.

"Go on then." She says and waves her hand at the space stretched out in front of us, in response to my raised brow. I stare at her for a long moment before tentatively getting to my feet and moving forward.

The ground that had been soft to sit on, hardened to a wooden dance floor as I walk over it. The girl who had been dancing by herself saw me moving hesitantly and paused to wave me over. I went to her and she curtsied without a word; I bowed to her and then she stepped closer and we began to move. With music playing around us, we didn't need to speak—we connected in our movements; a purer connection than trying to find the right words anyway. I couldn't explain how I knew the choreography but my body flowed through it like I'd been practicing this dance for years—in a way perhaps I had. As we moved, my steps pulled deep purple flowers from the ground showing on the mirror, hers sprouted the exact pink of her leotard.

She went still beneath my hands suddenly, before her head snapped over to the mirror. Her hand grabbed mine and together we ran till we stood just before the mirror—I noted that these steps didn't produce any flowers and then something else stole my attention. A little boy was chasing a younger girl through the field, laughing and squealing as they went. Behind them, an adult couple strolled more peacefully about the flowers, hands clasped between them. A picnic basket was set down and a blanket spread before they called to their children. The woman spoke to the little girl about how pretty the flowers were and I smiled. Looking down on the little family, the dancing girl and I stayed still for a while.

Eventually, though, the music called us to motion once more.

The Child

Up on my tippty-toes I sneaked out into the room from behind the big, white, pushy door. My nose scrunched up at the too-cleanly smell so I pinch my eyes shut and shook my head around to not sneeze. Never liked that smell or the scary bright white walls. Don't like the way everybody looks all sad at you like everything is already over, no matter how many times they see you again. And extra-specially do not like all the pokey, sticky things everyone here carries around with them. Bad use for pockets if you ask me, always liked to keep candy in mine. Well, when mommy didn't catch me, have to pay attention now so I don't break Daddy's rules.

Don't be seen, that's the rules. Well except when you can be seen…then it's okay. But otherwise don't be seen and don't be heard and don't make a ruh-roo-row-ruckusth. Sneezing will get me seened I think. Seems rouckusthy to me. Anyway them's the rules. Be sneakity. That's what He said. Sneaker in an don't be seen except when you should be seen but mostedly don't be seened. Easy-peasy.

Closer. Just a little-itty-bit closer. I go still all over when my tenny-shoe makes a little squeaky noise on the floor but no one else seems to notice so I keep creeping, making sure to pick my toes all the way up off the floor and set them back down really extra carefully. There she is.

I step up to press my hands against the glass separating us. She's so little and so much too quiet. Eyes squeezed tight-tight the little thing looks like she'd cry if she had the energy. Her skin is rubbed red and bruised in a few places; she's been through so much in such a short time. All sorts of colors of tubes and wires are stuck with tape to her little body, even one going into her nose—I bet that smells even worser than the room. I raise my eyes to the tall man standing on the other side of the baby-display-case-thingy. His eyes are icky, bright red; his face quickly rubbed dry each time a new tear falls. He has one hand inside the baby's box and it's resting carefully—just the tippty tips of his scuffed fingers—on her little back. There's something in the look on his face, something I know because I've seen it before—just before I came here.

Her daddy is looking at her like she's the best thing in the whole world—the same way our Daddy in heaven looks at all of us. He says that we're pray-shuss. I'm not sure what it means but this daddy thinks his baby girl is pray-shuss too, I thinks. No wonder He sent me here. Pray-shuss things are supposed to be cared for because they are loved the most. That's what Daddy back home always says. He told me we're all pray-shuss and that's why He loves us and that love is when no matter what you want to protect something and make sure it's happiest as it can be.

He sent me here because this little baby needs some extra love and it needed delivering. Because her mommy tried to hurt her the same way my mommy tried to hurt me. Daddy doesn't want her to be sicky the way I gots sicky and had to spend so much time in this smelly place because of it. So, He sent me to come help. He knows I'll be extra careful with her because I know how bad it is to not be wanted. But she is wanted. Her daddy and Daddy want her to live.

I step around the box to the side with the touching hole in it and squeeze in, next to the sad-daddy-man. He doesn't look at me or tell me I'm not 'upposed to be here so I get up on my tippted-toes again and poke my arm into the hole in the box where the man's hand is. The baby doesn't respond when I brush my hand over the soft little curlies on her head so I pull my arm back and dig in my pocket for the little box He gave me.

Sticking my hand back into the hole, I dump the box over the little girl's head. A lonely drop of light—like water-sunlight—falls out of the box. The miracle splats all over her and her eyes open up. They're sky blue—not like the one in the cray-non box but like the one when your mommy wakes you up real early so, you can be to the doctors on time and even the sun doesn't want to be awake yet but it's light out anyway. She watches me, blinking slowly. I grin as her nose scrunches a bit, knew that tube couldn't smell no good. She stares as I move back and pat her daddy's hand gently in goodbye. My job here is all done with, I wait a little bit anyway to watch, as she wiggles and scoots over onto her side to grab at her daddy's hand, her itsy-bitsy fingers wrapping around his.

He doesn't bother wiping his tears anymore and his hand shakes against hers. Colored lights shine into the room from the small window across the room. A rainbow smiling down at us—Daddy smiling down at us. I head in the other direction from the rainbow where a wooden door swings open and skip back to home.

The Lost

In. Out…2, 3…again. When I'm breathing normally again, I look over my radio for new damage. I didn't crack anything this time; lucky me—ha. I'm not sure how much more it's going to survive before I'm stuck driving in silence but I can't help it. That song comes on and I just…in…I…I can't. The air sticks in my lungs again till I'm gasping against the suffocating pressure. Some part of my brain screams at me to calm down and slow my breathing but I don't remember how. That stupid fucking song; I don't even know why she liked it. Bunch of caterwauling if you ask me—ha, like she cared what anyone else thought of her music or anything else. Damn it! My head bounces a bit when it slams into the steering wheel but it doesn't shake her loose. Nothing has and I don't think anything is ever going to.

The blare of a horn behind me prompts my head up and I hold my hand out the window, middle finger up, for a moment as I push down on the gas pedal. A dark car speeds past me once we're through the light only to slam on its breaks a moment later to avoid smashing into a car stopped at the next red light. Where they thought they were going to get in standstill, bumper-to-bumper traffic anyway, I have no idea.

Staring at the bumper in front of me until my eyes burn from the light reflecting off the overly polished chrome, I consider turning my radio back on. On the one hand, I've got at least a twenty-minute drive left ahead of me—honestly who knows how long in traffic like this. On the other, without any noise I have to think and…well. Yep, radio it is. I flip stations until the harsh screeching of a heavy metal band fills the cab of my truck. I'm not a fan but neither was she and that's what important right now. I have no idea what they are saying, actually I think it might be a different song now…oh, who cares. I crank the volume up until the ruckus drowns out the horns and squealing breaks outside and my head is too numb to think—the way I like it these days.

The drive from campus to my tiny studio apartment takes a record hour and a half and I arrive more than ready to just fall into bed and sleep. After parking my truck in my assigned spot and making sure the pass is clearly visible on my review mirror so I don't have to fight with management again, I lock my truck and start the hike up to the fourth floor. I shake my head, a smile tugging at my lips as I remember the way she would insist on running up all forty-eight stairs. She would fall panting and laughing against my door as I chased her, taking steps two and three at a time. Now, it feels impossible to reach the top. My legs get heavier with every step and I reach my floor unable to breath in a way that has nothing to do with the effort of climbing the stairs.

My shoes scrape the old, rough carpet as I make my way to my door. The building isn't the best but the structure's sound and the locks hold so I don't mind. It's not very close to campus but I have a good truck and a decent job not too far away so that's okay too. Rent is cheaper here than closer to campus so that's nice but it had nothing to do with why I chose this place. No, it all came down to one thing. The landlord here said I could paint the walls, however I liked.

The tired hinges creak when the heavy door rocks back-and-forth as I fight to free my key from the weary lock. An ugly little puff of gray, black, white, and orange fuzz latches onto my jeans and rides the back of my leg into the kitchen. The little thing lets loose a gurgling bray as I catch his scruff and lift him up to set him on the counter. Rubbing himself on my hand, he starts to shake and make a sputtering droning that used to make me think he was broken—turns out he thinks he's purring. Right on cue he sneezes, before once again picking up the noise only to sneeze again as he somehow tickles his own nose in expressing his pleasure. I never wanted a cat but when he clawed the shit out of her parents, I couldn't just let the little mess go to the shelter. So, now I make sure he has water in his bowl before lifting him off the counter and try to set him on the floor. Notice, I said try.

Clinging to my sleeve until I pick him back up, Archimedes—yes, she named him that because apparently he's part owl—climbs up my arm until I have a fur ball perched on my shoulder and nestled into my neck. He splutters out a purr when I reach up and scratch between his ears as I make my way to my bedroom. Careful not to crush the cat, because who knows what kind of terrible noise he'd make then, I drop into bed. I curl onto my side and pull my phone from my back pocket.

Archimedes moves from the side of my neck onto the bed, kneading the worn sheets a bit before curling against my chest and looking up at me with his pale, yellow eyes. He gives a cough noise I assume is supposed to be a meow so I respond like he articulated himself as well as he thinks he did.

"How was your day, Arch?" I question quietly.

Huff, huff, squeak, sneeze.

"Oh wow, that's pretty cool. You did all that by yourself huh?"

Merf-pluh, and a little nose lick—his own nose of course, not mine.

"Well I'm impressed, Arch. Sounds like you had a pretty busy day, little guy." I scratch a single finger under his jaw and he leans into my hand before responding.

Yawn. Stretch. Putter-putter. Huff.

"Yea my day was pretty good, I missed you too." Rolling onto my back I pull him so he lays on my chest. He puffs indignantly but settles quickly, gnawing on one of my old, dark-blue hoodies' strings. "That's not for eating, Arch." Uninterested he ignores me and continues chewing on my jacket. Whatever.

I lift my phone from where I had dropped it on the bed and slide the screen open so I can see her face. A bright smile looks back at me, she was always smiling like that. I don't think she knew she had paint on her nose but honestly, she probably just didn't care. I let my head fall to the side so I can look at the pictures of the two of us in the frame on my nightstand. In the biggest one I had come to pick her up for prom our senior year. Decked out in a suit with a bouquet of bright yellow daisies, she'd answered the door in a baggy t-shirt and a pair of cut-off shorts. Covered in paint, her eyes had gone wide and I'd thought she was going to cry. I remember her hugging me when I just laughed. The picture shows the paint stains she'd left all over the rental suit.

The other she gave me for my last birthday. It was taken just before I asked her to marry me. We'd been in her parents' back yard—I was pushing her on the old wooden swing that still hung from their large oak tree. I had caught the ropes when she swung backward and she fell against my chest trying to keep her balance. Laughing she had turned to look at me—so close our noses almost touched—and we stayed there for a moment just watching each other. I hadn't even known her mom was outside to take the picture; hadn't found out until she'd squealed like a stuck pig when I slipped a ring on her daughter's finger. She still wore that ring but I had never gotten the chance to give her the second one.

I looked past the pictures to the mural she had painted on the wall. Deep greens and browns blended into pine trees so real you could almost walk into them. My gaze traveled across the room to the wall facing my bed where a large abstract of warm yellows and reds blazed. Above my head, glow-in-the-dark paint allowed her to compose constellations that only come out on the midnight-blue background when the room is dark. My whole apartment is like that; every available space blocked out and painted at least once. A few of the walls she'd painted over and redone a time or two. That's why I'd needed an apartment where I could paint the walls—so she could decorate them for me.

Tracing the bright lines of my—our—personal stars with my eyes, I press down the first speed dial on my phone. The ringing sends a chill down my spine and Archimedes head raises off my chest, a concerned ear twitch coming my way when the shudder runs through me.

1. 2. 3. 4. 5. 6.

And then she's there. Her voice filling the room the same way it used too. This is the reason I keep paying her phone bill—I can't let go of this just yet. I can't lose her voice; can't forget the way she laughed or said my name; the way she said every word; how her voice lit up like every other part of her when she spoke about art; I can't forget her. I *won't*.

"Hey, Trey. I'm in the studio, sorry. Come get me or I'll call you back later. I love you, baby."

That's all her voicemail had to say. Nothing about leaving a message because I was the only person who ever actually called her and she'd rather I just came and saw her in person anyway. Her parents had put all the paintings —I couldn't fit in my apartment—in storage and dropped the lease on her little studio they had rented to get the smell of paint out of their house.

1. 2. 3. 4. 5. 6.

"Hey, Trey. I'm in the studio, sorry. Come get me or I'll call you back later. I love you, baby."

She says my name like it's something special—like I'm someone special. I never could convince her she was wrong.

1. 2. 3. 4. 5. 6.

"Hey, Trey. I'm in the studio, sorry. Come get me or I'll call you back later. I love you, baby."

Archimedes snuffs at my face and I realize the stars have blurred above me.

1. 2. 3. 4. 5. 6.

"Hey, Trey. I'm in the studio, sorry. Come get me or I'll call you back later. I love you, baby."

"I love you too, Braelynn."

The Faithless

I was on my feet before I was fully awake, rushing to the front door with my heart pounding a rapid pattern in my chest. I twist the door handle hard, only beginning to catch my panting breath after the fifth or sixth jerk on the unyielding metal. Turning my back to the thick, wooden door, I slide down until I hit the ground, feeling the scratch against my bare shoulders all the way. My eyes stray to the door down the hall—half hidden at this angle; I can't see the bloody hand print stained deep into the stark white paint.

I haven't opened that door. How can I? I don't deserve to step foot in her space.

Her accusations still ring in my ears.

I wish I'd listened; believed her.

Mine wasn't the hand that had left that crest emblazoned on her door but all the same I killed her.

My own daughter. I let her go through Hell because I didn't believe her.

I might as well have left that stain; I sealed her fate to it when I left a similar mark on her cheek the first time she told me what he did.

Tears I don't deserve to cry slide down my cheeks as I choke on sobs. I want to scream; to beg forgiveness as I break down into the tears I fight so hard; more than anything

I just want to say her name but I gave up that right when I didn't trust her. When I let that man into our home no matter how she cried. When I let him kill her and all the times I let him touch her.

I wish I could say I didn't know, maybe then I could find some kind of peace. I can't say that though. Can't even lie to myself when the way she begged me to listen just plays in my mind every time I try.

My little song bird.

A sob breaks through my clenched jaw when I remember the way I told her to just give up on her dreams. "You'll never amount to anything if you keep wasting your time on music," I said. And oh, how she cried when I smashed her violin against the wall. The only thing I ever wanted for her was to have a better life than the one I could give her and instead I broke her; let him destroy her.

My heart tugs at my mind telling me to pray; ask forgiveness, it beats out but I don't deserve that. After all I've done I have no right to even ask for mercy.

She was only a child. My Child. My Baby. My Dreamer.

My Nika.

And I ruined her.

The Anticipated

I winced as the tube in my left arm shifted when I scratched at the tape holding it in place but didn't stop.

"How many times do I have to tell you not to scratch at those?" The nurse—currently on duty—snaps at me as she rushes into the room to adjust the instruments I've shifted while trying to get comfortable.

"Oh, I figure at least one more. Unless, of course, you've brought less itchy tape." I try to joke but I know it falls dry. It's hard to keep a positive attitude when you're in pain twenty-four-seven though so I'll forgive myself this once. The nurse just rolls her eyes, not taking the bait and huffs off to bother someone else. "Rude," I call after her, knowing I won't get a response. Settling back into the bed hurts but not as much as trying to support myself so I grit my teeth until I'm leaning back against the soft-ish hospital pillows.

It's hard to keep my eyes open so I close them but don't sleep. I have to stay awake to see Luke, he said he had news to tell me. I force my eyes open again and slowly turn my head to look at the clock on the wall with a groan. He should be here by now.

"Would you quiet down over there?" My roommate calls out, sounding as agitated as ever.

"Oh yeah, my bad, sorry didn't mean to annoy you with my sounds of pain. I'll try to be more respectful." I call back with a roll of my eyes. Ugh! Even that hurts anymore.

I watch the clock click rather than go through the pain of moving my neck again. The pad of sensible shoes reaches my ears followed by hushed voices. My roommate is probably complaining about me again.

"Mr. Halle, why do you have to antagonize the other patients?" I laugh before I can stop myself and immediately regret it; not because of the affronted look on her face of course. No, that's hilarious actually—but because of the agony that kind of motion sends shooting through my entire body. My chest aches, my lungs somehow throbbing, and I feel like someone dropped a truck on me.

"I did nothing of the sort, ma'am." I say as soon as I can without pushing it between gritted teeth.

"She says you implied she has no compassion, again." The grumpy nurse whose name I refuse to remember looks even more frustrated than usual. I'd grin if it didn't take so much effort.

"I'm afraid I just don't know what you're talking about, Eliza."

"You never do." She sighs, "And my name is Emily." She scowls at me.

"Well I was close." I say with as much cheer as I can muster up in my voice, though I still don't force my muscles to form a smile. In response, she throws her hands up and promises the lady in the other bed that she'll see if there are any vacancies in other rooms before stomping out.

"Bye-bye, Lily." I holler after her to the annoyance of my roommate if her loud, drawn-out sigh is any indication.

44

If I could open the curtain between our beds, I'd do it; just to annoy her more. Fortunately, for her trying to stand is beyond my pain threshold at the moment.

Gritting my teeth, I settle into bed once more, silently cursing the cancer infecting my bones. Ugh. As if that wasn't bad enough, the doctor says the real worry is the cachexia; I found out from a google search on my phone that cachexia is also called "Wasting Syndrome" and is common in bone cancer victims. So, basically my entire body is falling apart. She says if it spreads to my heart there won't be anything they can do to keep that muscle from deteriorating as well; I'm still waiting for information on what they're doing for the rest of it actually. My muscles are atrophying; I can now count my ribs with a glance, because both the wasting disease and the chemo ruin my appetite; and my doctor warned me to be careful because my bones have gotten so weak, I could break one of those newly visible ribs with little effort. I'm so tired.

Luke should be here by now. I open my eyes to look at the door when it opens, excited to see him, but it's only the nurse from earlier here to wheel my roommate to a "more comfortable environment." I close my eyes again when she glances at me. I'm too tired to argue anymore today. I just want to see Luke. I told the doctor that my chest has been hurting and she said we'd run some tests later today. I hope Luke gets here in time to hold my hand. Always makes me feel better when he's here to hear the bad news with me. She looked worried; when a doctor looks worried about something a kid dying of cancer says bad news is coming. Okay, worse news.

I hear the door snap closed behind my ex-roommate but don't open my eyes to look at the empty space she'd been in. Someone new would show up soon enough and I'd probably bother them into asking for a move too. She was my sixth roommate after all. I think it bothers them watching someone so young dying without much hope of recovery at this point. That's why they normally seclude children in their own hospitals; people don't like to see children hurting. This hospital was closer to Luke's dance studio so I wanted to go here instead of the Children's Mercy Hospital across town. My parents didn't care where I went as long as I was getting treated and they could keep pretending I was coming home soon. I wonder which is harder—watching your son die or hearing your dad's muffled sobs against your bed when he thinks you're asleep after your mom couldn't "take anymore" and walked out of the hospital without looking back.

Concentrating, I force my mind to happier times and can almost hear Luke's laugh in my ears. I haven't heard it in a long time; his real laugh left with my diagnosis just like our mother. He fakes one for me as often as he can and I don't tell him I can hear the tears in it. It's how we are now; how we have to be. I picture the two of us playing catch with an old football in our back yard. Neither of us were very good so it was more like a mutual game of fetch but it was a lot of fun. Laughing at each other for our terrible passes and fumbles we'd stayed outside until we couldn't see each other anymore. Sunburned and tired, we'd stumbled inside to find mom and dad dancing in the kitchen as they finished cooking dinner together.

Together; that's the best way to describe my family before all this happened. You could always look at my parents and see how in love they were. Luke and I were the best of friends, even though I was a few years younger than him. I don't know how to describe us anymore. Tired, maybe. Luke trying to hold my dad and me, both up. My dad doing everything he can for both of us and trying to keep himself from breaking down. Me wasting away to nothingness in this stupid bed. Yea, I think tired is our new word.

I know I'm tired.

I feel myself falling asleep and fight a losing battle to stay awake. I hope Luke wakes me up when he gets here.

Shifting through dreams of happier times and things that never happened-but make my dream-self smile just the same, I suddenly feel myself getting lighter. Looking down, I see my body is fading away, translucent as all the pain I've felt just floats away. I lift my gaze and Luke is smiling at me. His body is fading into transparency as well; his grin open and honest for the first time in a long time. He holds his hand out to me and I see a brilliant light behind him shining through his faded body. I step forward, settling my hand into his and he leads me to the light.

We step through together and a comforting warmth settles deep into my soul, washing away even the deepest memory of pain. Tears spill over my cheeks, my mouth pulled into a wide smile as I feel the most comforting sensation wrap around me. I feel safe and loved as I am engulfed in the soft light, it's like coming home; like a hug after a hard day, spending time with your family when the whole world seems to be falling apart; like all these things and so many more but also nothing like them at all. It's a feeling I will never be able to explain to someone who hasn't experienced it; like every bad thing never happened and you're experiencing all the good at once. It's the feeling you get when He claims you as His own and you feel His love in every fiber of your being for the first time; but so much stronger, knocking me to my knees as I welcome the tenderness into my soul in a way I never could while still ensnared in my old body.

And then everything goes dark.

The Tempest

Every pounding step echoed in the soaked air. Breaths were gasps; desperate pants against the suffocating weight. Breathing was drowning in a storm like this. I clung desperately to the slick, soaked reigns; head tucked into my horse's warm neck, I prayed she could find her way home in this downpour.

A sudden flash of light spooked us both and I felt more than heard thunder ripple through the air. Another flash and the warmth of my mare disappeared from beneath me. I tried to scream but the next roll of thunder swallowed my voice; as I hit the ground, darkness swallowed my vision; and in the space of a wild, final heartbeat the storm swallowed me.

***

The next thing I know my horse is nudging me awake. Her soft lips nestle against my cheek before she moves up to pull at my hair and huff in my face. I move cautiously—not sure if I broke anything—to rub my fingers against her jaw. A low whinny and a brushing of lips over my nose greet my searching hand and a smile automatically tugs at my lips, as I pry my eyes open.

I squint against the harsh light and stare at the strange horse in front of me. Slowly, I look over the large creature while she watches me with the same wary care. Then, as though she can't contain herself any longer, she neighs and dances back a few steps, her head jerking up and down at me impatiently.

Chuckling slightly, I get to my feet and step toward her, hands outstretched but before I can get very close, she steps forward and buts her head hard against my chest knocking me down. I glare up at her until it registers in my mind that cracking my tailbone on even water-soaked ground should have hurt a lot more than that. I look around to see soft grass surrounding me. It's long enough to curl around my legs and doesn't quite reach the tops of my boots when I get back on my feet. It's cool but dry beneath my hands with no mud pushing up between the sleek, polished blades.

This time she waits for me to come to her, nudging her nose more firmly into my hand when my fingers brush over it. Keeping that hand there, I step even closer and bring the other up to run through her soft mane.

As pure white as the rest of her, her mane is like silk wisping between my fingers. I brush my hand down from her mane to the side of her neck then to her flank till I reach a saddle. Her clear blue eyes tell me she's not an albino but she doesn't have any color on her except her hooves. They're solid gold.

Okkaaaaaayyy…

I'm either dreaming…or dead.

A pale blue blanket, the same color as her eyes is neatly folded under a worn-dark-leather saddle. It's just like my own saddle—as are her reigns—except for a spark of gold near the saddle's horn. Leaning close, I read the scrawling cursive words.

"Tempest? Is that your name, pretty-girl?" A whinny answers me but it doesn't come from the horse I'm standing against.

My head snaps up to meet the eyes of a rider a little way away. His horse is the same pure white as Tempest and he waves for me to come along before turning his horse in the other direction. I pull myself easily up into the familiar saddle and Tempest is moving before I'm sure we should follow him. I let her go to him though, something in my gut telling me to trust him. Rather than letting me stop beside him, the rider starts his horse moving when we reach him and Tempest paces herself beside them.

"Well, hello there, little lady, it's nice to meet you." The deep drawl rumbles from his chest at odds with his surprisingly gentle grey eyes.

"Nice to meet you too, sir, can you tell me where we are though?" I question, looking up at him when he chuckles at me.

"No need for that sir stuff, darling, name's Phil. And as for where we are, I think you already know that one." He raises a brow at me and I nod, understanding. I was already kind of assuming that was the case anyway.

"Well at least that explains the gold hooves." I mutter. Loud laughter rips from Phil at my comment and I can't help the smile that crosses my lips.

"Threw me at first too, girl." He says between belts of laughter. "Anyways," he says when he manages to sober up a bit, "you got a name or do I have to keep calling you girl?"

"Tally, sir." I tell him.

"What did I say about that sir nonsense, Tally?" He has a mischievous glint in his eye as he glares down at me.

"Right, sorry, Mr. Phil." He snorts and shakes his head. "Alright, smart mouth, let's get this show on the road." He nudges his horse to move a bit faster and Tempest follows them so I just let her have her reign.

The faster we run the louder the air around us gets, igniting a buzzing deep in my veins. Thunder chases the sound of our horses pounding steps. Electricity crackles in the air, breaking overhead as Phil's horse lets out a loud whinny. Before long we're drenched in the rain we're creating and I can't help but throw my head back and laugh loudly. There's no fear in this storm.

We reach the edge of the clouds the field we're in is on, and Tempest comes to an easy stop along the edge. The storm doesn't stop but continues out over the edge. Looking down, I catch a glimpse of Earth below; our storm soaking the air and ground beneath that.

"What'd ya think, kid?" Phil asks when the thunder is far enough away, we don't have to yell over it anymore.

"I've never ridden a horse as fast as Tempest before." I couldn't have kept the grin off my face if I'd tried. I didn't try.

"Who?" Phil asks.

"Tempest." I repeat, leaning forward to stroke her neck as I speak, "It was on her saddle." I continue. Phil chuckles kindly in response.

"That ain't the horse, Tally." He tells me.

"Then what is it?" I frown at him.

"It's you, darling. You're the storm; the rain maker; the Tempest."

I smiled when I thought about it. The storm may have taken me at first but I don't have to be afraid anymore.

Now I am the storm.

The Catalyst

The car was hers but he drove. One hand on the wheel and the other gripping her hand in between them—he rubbed his thumb over the ring, he'd place on her finger. He grinned as she sang along to a song he didn't know. She was a painter not a singer. He laughed at her out of key attempts at rhythm.

It was the last thing she heard.

An impossible weight brought the small, blue car to a sudden and devastating stop. The hood crumpled under the pressure of the truck that had hit them head on; the dash folded into the passenger seat, the steering wheel catching on the center console. Glass rained over them from the destroyed windshield a moment before everything went still.

The truck had come to rest with one tire through the windshield of the smaller vehicle, by some miracle the structure of the roof had held rather than caving in on the couple. He looked up at the undercarriage of the pick-up and tried to catch his breath—before he had, he was screaming.

He was still begging her to answer when flashing lights and uniforms surrounded him. The driver's door had to be cut open so he could be pulled out with the weight of the truck compacting the latch on the door. He would need stitches where glass had stuck in his chest but it wasn't deep enough to cause any internal damage. His arm had been badly burned either by the tire or the air-bag, he wasn't sure and he didn't care. He tried to push his way around the car but the paramedics held him back dragging him into an ambulance. He called her name—desperate for any response—until they sedated him in the hospital.

She wouldn't answer. She couldn't answer. Her seat belt hadn't functioned properly; allowing her to fall forward. She would have gone through the windshield but the air-bag deployed fine. The force threw her back and fractured her neck. She died instantly.

The other driver stumbled from his truck without a scratch; too drunk to remember the incident the next day.

The Repose

"I told you to keep quiet, didn't I?" The man's voice was deceptively calm as he pushed the door shut behind him and slid the lock into place. "Wasn't that much to ask, I don't think. Just keep your stupid little mouth shut but it was too much for you, I guess. Should've known, you wasn't that smart."

Crouched carefully behind a scuffed guitar, its ragged case, an assortment of mostly-malfunctioning music stands and an old beat-up amplifier, the girl he was addressing couldn't help but shake; her hand clamped hard over her mouth to muffle her panicked breathing, she couldn't stop the tears falling from her eyes any more than she could slow the rapid beating in her chest. She knew too intimately how heavy the man's hands could be.

"I know you're in here, Sweetheart." The man continued in a low, steady voice as he made his way to the closet. "Might as well come on out, you're just gonna piss me off trying not to fess up to your crimes, stupid girl." The closet was left wide open as he knelt to look under the bed.

The man looked around as he rose from the floor and his eyes landed on the small figure huddled in the corner. With a grin that had sent a tremor down the girl's spine more times than she could count, he starts toward her without making a sound. Grabbing a handful of her hair, the man drug her out from the haven her music had tried to create. He silenced her scream by throwing her to the floor in the center of the room. Reaching back, he palmed the neck of her guitar as he stalked toward her shaking form.

"Never did know how to be quiet did you, Sweetheart?" The girl tried to scramble backward to the door but he was already stepping closer. "Always playing that worthless music…well let's see how well you like your instruments now."

With that, he brought the guitar around and smashed it against her—sending the music stands and everything balanced on them flying. Blood pooled from her head but she managed to struggle to her feet, as he stumbled clumsily backward at the force of the swing. She made for the door again but the heavy weight of a second swing caught her between the shoulders and she came up hard against the wall instead—staining the stark white paint red with her blood.

The third swing came just as she was pushing herself off the wall and threw her in the opposite direction. Before she could catch her balance, yet another blow knocked her off her feet and she crashed to the floor—her head bouncing off the solid oak bed frame before she crumpled completely. The man took the pleasure of kicking her solidly in the stomach a few times before stepping firmly between her shoulders on the way out the door but it was a wasted effort.

She was already gone.

The Delay

The young man stepped through the door with his friends' laughter still surrounding him. He glances back at them and shakes his head as they playfully shove at each other. He steps fully outside and lets the door swing shut behind him. He has a more important place to be and he's already running late.

He'd stayed too long, borrowing strength from his fellow dancers. His long-time friend and dance partner had pled for just one more song at least four times. His heart more at peace as they danced than it had been in longer than he could remember, he'd been unable to deny her request. They'd moved from the challenging steps of the dance they were honing for a competition next month to the familiar choreography of dances they had been doing for years. Ending with an upbeat add-lib waltz, they laughed as they both tried to one up each other's best moves. Out of breath, they'd leaned against each other as they headed for the showers—he insisting it was time to go.

The shot came from a passing truck that never even slowed down. The driver screamed some sort of insult out of the window that he didn't understand. His friends heard the word faggot ringing in the air a moment before the gunshot, as they came through the door behind him. The injured dancer stumbled back against the others; dark blood soaking his pale gray shirt. He heard their screams as his blood smeared their clothes and skin as he was sinking against them to the ground. He vaguely heard a frantic voice begging for an ambulance and knew it wouldn't do any good. His limbs grew heavy and he tasted blood as he tried to say his brother's name.

His little brother lay aching in a stiff bed twenty minutes away, waiting for him to come. The twelve-year-old wanted to see his brother one last time as badly as the bleeding seventeen-year-old wants to see him. The young man's friend shushed him when he tried to say his brother's name again, wanting the other man to tell his brother that he loved him. All that came from his mouth was a choked gasp and a gush of blood. He never heard the sirens of the ambulance coming to rush him to the same hospital his brother laid in. He never got to his little brother.

They would see each other soon.

The Unexplainable

Things happen, every now and then, that no one can explain. Things that just don't really make sense. Things that defy all odds or even science. Some people call these things coincidence or chance, they're known to others as luck and fate. Those that understand how these un-understandable things happen though, the ones who know to call upon the Lord in their time of need and recognize when He answers such prayers for others as well—they call them miracles. One such event involved a young girl with little chance at living after her mother attempted an abortion, a father who would do anything for his daughter—who pled for a second chance, and a Father who always had a plan.

The girl was cradled now in the arms of her dad, her gaze fastened to his face. It was the first time he'd been allowed to hold her since she was born and although the nurse said she could not stay out of her incubator long, it was the greatest moment of his life. His precious baby girl—whose own mother had tried to murder her—grasping his finger in her too tiny hand. She was months premature after the doctor had tried to poison her, destroying the nutrients in the womb around her but not managing to kill her.

The greatest miracle he had ever witnessed was his little girl surviving so that he could have this chance to hold her. This chance to watch her grow up and become the beacon of God's light and mercy, he knew she would someday be. Most importantly to him, he was given the chance to love her; but even he didn't know the potential his daughter would have.

The Lord indeed had great plans for this child; His grace had saved her from death and His love would guide her in the life she would now have. The father smiled down at the little girl in her incubator after the nurse said she needed to return to it. Heart calming as the nurse said that his daughter was as healthy as she could be. Neither the girl's father nor the kind nurse could even begin to fathom the plans God had for this small soul. They could not know that one day not only would she herself be a doctor, working tirelessly to save the lives of others, but would also be an outspoken adversary of abortion. They could not know that the attempted abortion would leave her unable to have children—leading her to adopt three children who were also not wanted by their own mothers. They could not even image that one of these three children would one day be on the team that cured cancer.

They could not know, but He did.

The Sentinel

I'd probably have dropped my shoe by now if I'd been wearing one, they were never tied after all. I wonder what would happen if I did. Would it fall and hit someone? Could it even fall to Earth; I doubt it works that way but what do I know?

The sky keeps changing as I look through the giant curved lens of it to the Earth far below. I swing my feet slowly in the nothingness as I wait. I'm not sure anymore how long I've sat here or how long I'll have to keep sitting here; but I know I'm not leaving till I see him. I can't explain when or why the need to see him again hit me but I found myself here before I really knew where I was going.

"Hey, Braelynn, come, do the sunset with us," A familiar voice calls cheerfully from behind me.

"Not today," I say without even looking up. Not until I know why I needed to be here.

"Why not?" A different voice questions, curiously. It's a good question.

"I don't know," I tell them. I don't know what else to say; I have no clue how to try to explain this feeling. It's like I'm being told to do something except it's coming from inside me. I used to get a feeling like this sometimes when I painted; it was like someone else was guiding my brush for me—they were the best paintings I ever did. This is almost the same but so much stronger.

A loud, exaggerated sigh tells me they're leaving more than the quiet footsteps that come after. I know they aren't mad; they just don't understand my desire to be here—that's okay though, neither do I.

I roll my favorite paintbrush between my fingers idly as I watch a familiar truck pull to the curb next to a building, I think I recognize. Nothing about the Earth is all that memorable anymore—it's more like it was all a dream and now that I've woken up here, everything is so much more vivid.

Everything but him. I'll never forget him as long as I exist in any form. The way his fingers felt between mine; how the softness of his hair collapsed around my hand when I touched it; the way his laugh could fill a room; how he could fill every empty piece of me with just a smile; that look in his eyes when he told me he loved me—the tears that flooded them the first time I said it back; everything that he has ever been is burned so deeply into my soul that not even death could touch it.

He moves with a determined purpose up the steps into a room filled with paintings I once upon a time thought were art. Circling the room with slow strides, he comes to the painting he always said was his favorite. It's a portrait of the two of us but you can't see our faces at all. The perception is from behind and to the side of him. You can only see little glimpses of me where I'm wrapped around him and tucked into his embrace. He said he had to have it when I was finished so we hung it on the wall in his apartment and it never moved. He let me paint all the other walls with countless murals and abstract pieces but not that wall. It's still the ugly, off-white beige-ish color it was when he moved in, because he wouldn't let me take the portrait down to paint the wall. He would never even let me hang any other paintings on the wall because he said he wanted it to be the only thing you saw when you looked at it; because that's how he felt when he looked at me. The sap.

He steps closer to the painting and runs his hand across the strips of my painting hair that drape over his painting shoulder.

"I miss you, Lynn." He murmurs to the painting. I don't know how I can hear him—I've never been able to hear anyone down there before—and I don't care. Now that it washes over me, I realize how badly I've craved hearing his voice again.

"I miss you too, Trey. So much," I whisper, knowing somehow that he can't hear me.

"I'm so lost without you, baby. I don't know what to do anymore." He's still standing in front of the canvas but he drops his hand, letting it swing limply by his side. He looks down for a moment but his eyes rise quickly to trace over the lines of paint again.

"You'll be okay," I tell him. If only he could hear me too.

"I just want to be with you again." His voice is no more than a breath when he slides his hand beneath his shirt to pull a revolver from the back of his waist band. I stop breathing as he pulls it in front of him to fiddle at it like he knows what he's doing. When did he get a gun? Where did he get a gun? *Why*?

"Trey." I call out, begging for some sort of miracle. I can't watch this. Why would He make me come here to watch this? How could He let this happen? Frantic thoughts beat against my skull as I watch the love of my life and death lift the gun to his head. No. No, no, no, no. *Please*.

"I'm coming, Braelynn." He whispers with a smile pulling at his lips. His eyes fall closed and I watch his hand tense around the weapon.

"No!" I scream as loud as I can manage. Suddenly, I was on my feet from throwing myself forward off the cloud. I didn't fall to him though, another cloud forming from nothing beneath my feet. I was helpless to save him; I couldn't get any closer and he couldn't hear me from here.

His head snaps up as if he heard me though and we both watch as a violent wind forces the windows open and blinding sunlight suddenly floods the dark room. It burns over his skin stronger than sunlight could be on its own and the first tears I've cried since coming here fall as the pistol clatters to the ground. He steps closer to the window where the light is coming in from, letting the heavenly warmth surround him. Outside his apartment, rain pounds the pavement but inside brilliant light scorns the shadows and forces him to his knees. I watch him bow before his pain and reach for salvation.

On our knees, we cry together as I watch over him. Mine are tears of joy seeing the man I love find forgiveness, life, and hope. His, I know, are tears of relief. The pain slowly leaving his body as love—true, incomparable love—pushes it aside. I can't help but smile as I look down.

The light shining over him begins to change slowly at first then faster, a stunning display of indescribable color.

The rain around him dries up to nothing and like that he is standing at the end of a rainbow. A beauty and a gift only the Lord himself could create. Color unlike anything I have ever seen before—even in this miraculous place I reside now—spreads into even the deepest crevices of his apartment and his soul. Spears deep into my soul from so far away—undeniable love. It is a guarantee that love is greater than pain, greater than fear and that God is greater than the weight of loss plaguing Trey. It is a promise that I will see him again. A loving pledge to heal a hurting soul and bring him home to where he is loved; it is a promise.

I will see him again.

The Forgiven

The smashed television glares at me through the silence in the room. I hate silence but I've come to hate sound even more. She was always making sound; singing or humming; tapping her fingers; playing some sort of music. It was never quiet when she was still here—now it always is.

Rain pelts the windows and the dark walls light up with a crack of lightning. Thunder follows soon after and the rain turns into a down pour. I watch as it keeps coming down harder and harder. The next bout of thunder shakes pictures from the walls and I jump out of the way of falling glass. Harsh wind forces the windows open and just like that I'm in the storm rather than watching it happen outside. I try to get close enough to shut the elements out once more but rain quickly turns to hail and between that and the wind I'm backed into the hallway.

The turbulent wind follows me and in a hard-wet gust her door is thrown open. The first time it's been open in months and I can't help but stray toward it, distracted from the violent weather wrecking the house. I stop at the door, unable to get any closer to the destruction in the room. Smashed furniture is mixed with broken instruments that are stained by blood. Sheet music is flung about the room, covering everything like a white shroud. Everything except the walls, where streaks of darkened red tell of the battle that took place here.

The wind pushes into the room around me and lifts the pieces of music from where they've settled. The paper rattles around the room; rising into the air and flinging into the walls—held plastered over the stains by the forceful wind.

Once it has uncovered it, the wind finds the strings of the guitar left half smashed on the floor. I watch the strings shift as though fingers are pressed into them and music fills the room. I stumble closer, landing on my knees near the wreckage and watch the song form on the strings. The storm has gone silent but still, the strings move in the melody of the first song Nika ever learned to play for the choir at the church her teacher took her to. Her voice floats through my head like she's still here.

"A-maaay-ziiiing Graaace, how sweeeet the sound, tha-at saaaved a wretch like meeeee.

I once was looost but now am found,

Was bliiind but now I seeee.

Twaaaas Grace that taught my heart to fear

And Grace my fears reeliiiiieeeeved.

How preeeccious did that Grace appear

The hour I first beelieeeved.

You've got to believe, Mama. He's got enough Grace to cover you, but you have to believe first."

It's as if she's right there in the room with me—her gentle voice carried on the violent wind—and I finally let out the tears and screams of pain that I haven't let myself feel for her before. I don't deserve to grieve for my girl but it's no longer a choice. The guitar keeps playing and my daughter's beautiful voice circles around me as I bow my head and pray for the first time in far, far too long. I pray that my daughter is happy where she is; I pray that she and God both can forgive me for what I let happen; I pray that she gets to play her music in heaven; I pray for healing; I pray for strength and forgiveness. Warmth surrounds me as the storm slowly fades away and light fills the room. I can feel a presence pushing into the room around me, settling over and deep inside me as I kneel on the floor feeling love move back into my soul. Slowly trying to catch my breath and calm myself, I pray for comfort between pleas for forgiveness. Knowing I don't deserve it, I pray for a love only God can give.

From the open window there is suddenly light. Light, the likes of which does not exist here on earth—heavenly light like fire burning away my agony. Color bursts through the room painting the walls and staining deep within me. A rainbow searing the shadows and the bleak grays from my very soul. Decorating me in hope and faith and love—staining me deep as the blood on the wall. The heavier the light settles over me—settles into me—the lighter I become. The condemning weight on my shoulders and in my soul lifts away into this glorious light. Baptized and freed in the Lord's love.

I am washed in His Grace.

The Visitor

Grass scratched against my bare toes as I sat picking at a hole in the knee of my favorite jeans. The worn-soft denim surrendered a loose string to my efforts and I freed it to float on the light breeze. A little way off Luke moves gracefully with a girl I've met a few times—she seems nice—their motions mirrored behind them by flowers blooming on the screens that show the Earth far below.

I know I should worry about finding my own purpose here but I'm still getting hung up on how painless everything is. Moving is effortless and I can laugh without doubling over in pain. Just the thought has a smile pulling at my mouth and I let it because for the first time in so long, it doesn't hurt. Nothing hurts.

Luke's unrestrained laughter draws my gaze back to him and his partner, a smile tugging at my own mouth, as they move to music I can't hear. I watch them for a few moments before shifting my gaze further back to the mirror behind them. A man makes his way across a field dotted with large stones, decorated with flowers and small wooden crosses—he looks familiar.

Rolling easily to my feet brings a giddy smile to my face from pure reflex of anticipating pain and not feeling it. I make my way toward the mirror—careful not to get in the dancers' way. Reaching the screen, I watch the familiar man kneel before two of the ornate stones. He traces the lettering on the first stone lightly—as though he's scared of damaging it.

Lucas Omar Halle

"Hey Luke," I call over, "This rock has your name on it."

"What are you on about?" Luke asks, as he comes up beside me. He looks when I point to the mirror and the noise he makes is pained. Stepping even closer, he lifts his hand to rest on the glass over the man as he in turn reaches to trace the name on the other stone.

Elias Phillip Halle

"Eli," Luke chokes out, "that's our dad." My eyes widen at the knowledge and I don't dare look away from the man as he dusts the rotting flowers away and replaces them with new ones.

"I'm sorry, boys." Dad murmurs to the graves, his own voice filled with the same grief as Luke's. Reaching out, I take Luke's hand as we continue watching. "I love you, two. I'm sorry I didn't protect you better."

"We love you, too, Dad," Luke whispers, voice barely perceptible under our dad's loud sobs.

Without warning, the glass screen in front of us wavers and Luke's hand falls through to land on Dad's shoulder. Immediately, he steps forward but can't move any closer— only allowed this small touch. I reach forward hesitantly and my hand passes through the barrier as well, landing on Dad's other shoulder.

The moment we are both touching him, light and color explode all around us. Colors I have never seen or even imagined burst into and around us. Seeping deep into the three of us. A rainbow falling all around us and searing us closer than ever before. I can feel our dad's pain easing as our Father's love surrounds us in an incomprehensible beauty and burning light. I can feel that Dad knows that Luke and I are safe—that we are free. And I can feel that he too is going to be free one day—that he will survive this pain and he will join us here one day. I thought I had learned peace when I came here but I know it today. Here inside this light there is no thought, no feeling, but love.

Dad doesn't respond to the weight of our hands or the light falling on us but his breathing calms and although there are still tears in his eyes, he's no longer sobbing. We stand there as a family; separated and maybe a little broken but a family none the less as Luke and I watch over him.

"Love you, Dad. Always."

The Intruder

"Come on, Tally." The little hand kept tugging on mine, its owner showing no sign of answering my question anytime soon.

"But where are we going?" I asked for the fifth or sixth time. I followed along behind the small red-head without much of a fight but I was curious.

"I told you it's a thecret. You have to come doe because He said to take you."

"Where did He say to take me?" I shamelessly try to trick her into telling me.

"To the door. It's this way here." I can't believe that worked. Well, I guess she is only like five.

"What door?" I ask her as we continue walking quickly to where ever it is we're going. Well, she's walking pretty fast but it's actually really easy for me to keep up with her little legs.

"The one that leads to the other place so you can help the people." Oh, well that clears everything up.

"What?" Hey, you try getting information from a five-year-old sometime and see if it goes any better.

Heaving a deep sigh, she finally stops and turns to face me. She glares up at me like I'm being intentionally dense and to be honest it's both an adorable and an extremely unsettling look on such a young face.

"There's a boy who needses your helps," she says slowly while staring me right in the eye. "He is in the other place, the place we camed fromed."

"Okay." I nod along as she speaks, "so you're taking me to a door that leads to Earth?" I ask.

"Yes, now will you *come on*?" She asks with her little hands planted firmly on her hips.

"But why does he need my help?" She throws her hands in the air at my question and gives me an exasperated look which is more disturbing than anything on her chubby-cheeked face.

"How am I suppothed to know that? Daddy said to bring you so I'm bringing you." With that she turned and started walking again, correctly assuming I'd follow.

I follow her into an area I've never been before; trees close in around the path and the ever-present light seems to dim a bit, casting long shadows over us. The path narrows so that I have to walk a step behind her and the gold brick walkway fades into a rough cobble-stone path. The air begins to press down heavily on us like it didn't want us to be here. The further we went, the more it seemed like we weren't supposed to be here—like we were straying too close to something that wasn't meant for us to touch.

"Are you sure where you're going?" I asked the younger girl, unable to keep the nervousness from creeping over my tone—of all the places to trespass the afterlife didn't seem like the best choice.

"Yep, It's just a little bit more this way." Her little feet moved quicker as brighter light became visible up ahead. I don't think I was the only one who was getting a little freaked out back there.

I step after her into a small, brightly lit clearing. The cobble-stones are flatter here, laid more carefully with a pathway of golden bricks leading to the center of the circular area. At the end of the path is a door. Nothing stands around it just a simple wooden door. The grains of the wood stand out in random patterns looking worn but well kept. There's no handle on the door but a golden light is shining from the slightest crack beneath the door.

"Well, go on." I'm waved—rather impatiently—toward the door.

Stepping along the narrow path, I reach forward and a handle appears on the door. It swings open, the handle coming to meet my hand half way. Beyond the door is the other half of the clearing; looking through, I can see the golden bricks continuing toward the wooded area on the far side. I glance back to tell the girl I don't understand but she's already gone. With nothing else to do, I step over the bottom of the door and when my foot comes down it's not in the cobble-stone clearing but in a dark room that I don't recognize.

I look around and see art all over the walls—not hung there but murals actually painted on the walls. I spin a circle looking at the impressive pieces, not noticing the man in the room with me, until he speaks.

"I miss you, Lynn." I jump at the quiet voice and turn to see its owner stroking his hand along a canvas painting hung on the wall. It's the only art in the room that isn't painted directly onto the walls. It displays the same amount of talent as the others but there's an extra sort of passion to this one.

Like more care was put into its creation than the others. No, that's not exactly right. It wasn't that the artist had put more effort into the painting but that they perhaps put more feeling into it. The love between the subjects in the painting is clear, though you cannot see their faces. The delicate way his hand curves beneath her shoulder blade; the way she tucks herself snuggly into his side; his face tilted low enough to watch the expression on hers; her own hands are pressed flat against him, one on his back and the other near his rib cage. They're holding each other as close as possible and as the man in the room reaches to run a careful hand along the hair of the girl in the painting, I can see the same love reflected there.

"I miss you, too, Trey. So much." This voice is harder to find but I eventually look up to see a girl in a blue hoodie sitting on a cloud. I wave to her but she doesn't seem to notice me as she watches the man talk to his painting—or more likely, I'm guessing, her painting. Only the artists stray that close to the edges.

"I'm so lost without you, baby. I don't know what to do anymore." I flinch at the sound of his voice. It is the broken sort of painful that's hard to listen too. The hopelessness makes me cringe and my heart aches in my chest for this man I do not know.

"You'll be okay," the girl murmurs but I know he can't hear it. Her voice is desperate and pained. She can hear the devastation in his as well.

He rocks forward a bit on his feet, wavering. His head tilts forward to rest against the painting, his eyes squeezing shut. He shakes his head back and forth a bit. He's shaking, his breath coming in slow shuddering sobs. I want to comfort him but as I step forward, his eyes snap open and his head swings around so he's looking straight at me. I freeze as he watches me but when light flashes over his face, I realize he's not watching me at all—can't see me at all. He's watching the thunder storm in the window behind me. His lips twitch almost as though he's going to smile until another sharp sob is ripped from deep inside him. He turns his head back to the painting and lets his wet eyes fall closed again.

"I just want to be with you again." He breaths out against the painting as he pulls a revolver from his waist band.

"Oh, um. Hey, not okay, sir. What are you doing with that?" I question loudly but he doesn't hear me. Oh, of course not. Just like he can't see me. To him I'm not even here, but I must be here for some reason. Looking around, I search for a way to get his attention and see rain pelting roughly against the window panes. Lightning strikes close by and thunder rolls over his next choked sob.

"Trey." The girl calls out—voice filled with horror. She's panicking. I can understand that—so am I.

"Okay, Trey. That's a cool name. Let's not do anything we'll regret alright. Please." I can hear the panic in my own voice now but of course no one else—namely this Trey fellow—can hear me at all. I know He wouldn't send me here just to watch this. I believe that with all my soul, so why am I here? It has to be to help Trey, but how?

"I'm coming, Braelynn." I watch as he raises the gun to his temple but I turn to the windows before I can see anything else. I have to get his attention somehow. Lightning strikes even closer now; the resulting crash of thunder shaking the walls of the room, maybe even the foundation of the old building. That's it.

"No!" The scream pierces the air at the exact same moment I throw the large balcony windows wide open. Wind pushes me roughly back into the room and I tumble head over heels across the carpet into the far wall. I look for Trey and see him staring in shock at the rain beating into the room before the clouds part, separating the rain into twin sheets falling on the sidewalk below. But what captures all three of our attention is the unearthly light pouring into the room and surrounding Trey. The familiar, heavenly light makes me feel warm inside and I smile as Trey tumbles helplessly to his knees—his gun long forgotten.

As I watch the light ripples and buckles, lightening and darkening, and breaking apart into a healing barrage of wondrous color; red as deep a crimson as blood and as brilliant as a ruby sparkling unmined and untouched in the shadows of the ground; fierce and overpowering, breaking into the room and changing the very air inside. Love plowing into the room—into Trey—with the force of a freight train; love knocking the breath from his lungs in a startled gasp as he reaches out for hope he'd long forgotten; love flooding furiously into the room, into his reach.

Orange, like the sun itself falling from the sky to reach long-burning fingers into the room and cast its warmth over this hurting soul. The healing fire of hope pressing forward to sear into Trey, giving him the ability to look forward and the chance to move past this pain. His memory not washed away—because forgetting is not the same as healing—but his soul strengthened so that he can continue to live. So, he can remember the good times and not dwell on the miseries. So, he can spread God's glory in the world.

Yellows from the most pallid, delicate hue to the most vibrant illumination, the purest namesake of light itself falling soft and careful as the first glittering, untouched snow of the season. The glory of the Lord brought forward to heal and to strengthen; to comfort and fortify; to show that this too can be overcome. That so long as you stand for the Lord, He will stand behind you and nothing can stand in your way. That faith in His glory, His grace, is the greatest weapon He gave us to fend off any foe.

Verdant, shining, emerald green, a firm streak of faith pressing forward into the room—into Trey—unshakably beautiful in its strength. His heart is reformed in this light, his soul forged into a greater strength than before. He is reborn in this light as a new man. A man who is saved. Doubts are pressed firmly out and away from him like shadows always flee from light. He shudders as the weight of his pain and fears falls from his shoulders, surrendered to God's unending mercy.

Deep, absolute, briny, honest blue encased the room, bleeding in and cooling the rough flames of the reds and yellows. A comforting blanket banking the harsher glare that came before it. Softening and fortifying, the harsh blow of the miracle light, settling it deeper and ever deeper into Trey's soul. Into a place where it can be reached by none but God Himself. It becomes an irremovable and fundamental part of Trey. Grace is wrapping protectively around him, securing him in the safety of his new Lord's love.

Indigo crashes into the room in waves as a final rippling blow erasing any possibility of the light's failure and pressing any shadows—any fears—out of the room. And out of Trey as well. Fearless now, he raises his hands above him, crying out in praise of God; in thanks of his pain, his fear, his weakness being replaced in this light by comfort, love, and strength. Leaning now on the comfort God is giving him, he knows somehow deep in his heart that he has not lost anything. They will meet again. This boy and his artist watching over him from the clouds.

Lastly, loose gentle tendrils and ribbons of violet curl into the room, binding us to this moment. Tying God's love into the room, too tight to question. No longer is a struggle for a soul, the light now a promise, that even when the light fades the love will remain. Trey has become a born-again child of God. He is saved. One day the Lord will welcome him home.

Deep inside this rainbow, I can see the Lords grace more plainly than it has ever been laid before me. Joy and love flood into me even though this chromatic display of His glory isn't meant for me. I can feel it in every cell of my being. I am blessed to be included in this act of His mercy for Trey and his artist. Blessed to see and to feel the absolute love of God as it is spread further—gifted to a new soul.

Separate from the vibrant, colored lights, a plain hardwood door wavers in the only shadows left in the furthest corner of the room and I make my way toward it, smiling. I am no longer needed here. It's time for me to go home.

The door swings open to greet me and I don't need to look back to know Trey will be okay.

The Faithful

A painter that decorates the sky and watches over a healing soul, a dream she never knew she had and a duty she would never turn down. Faith staining her soul as deep as the paint on her hands and in her heart; she never questioned the love of God. Fearless in her quest, she paints bold lines—and brilliant hope—on the sky for the world to see and know God's boundless glory. She is rewarded for her faith in knowing she will be with her love again one day.

Faith is believing in what your heart knows to be true but your mind can't prove. It's fighting for what you cannot see but that you can feel in your soul. Faith is complete trust and unwavering confidence. Loyal. Accurate. Honest. Reliable. Faith is the concrete that connects a soul to God and holds us steady and firm under any pressure.

The Hopeful

A musician who gives voice to a tuneless dance and comforts savaged hearts. Wearing hope like a second skin, her music calms the hearts and frees the minds of souls in need. She delivers peace to those whose names she will never need to know. The Lord's praise is sung in every note—every movement—that she makes. She is comforted in knowing that her mother is finding her own hope.

Hope is trusting that the light is greater than the darkness. It's believing that good will conquer—that God will Conquer—all. Hope is the undeniable expectation that miracles are happening all around you. It is the lens that lets you see the impact of these miracles on the lives they touch. Hope is the foundation of an honest soul and the purity of an open mind. Hope gives way to faith and dreams are born.

The Strong

A dancer who guides the motions of beauty in the world below; color and beauty bloom as he follows His lead. God's majesty is woven like light amongst the darkness in the world as he moves—planting life along the most hidden paths. He spreads beauty and hope to those willing to look in the least likely of places. His heart is warmed in knowing his Father will keep his father strong.

Strength of the heart and of the soul are forged in love and are boundless in their capabilities; ever-growing and reaching out to touch the lives of those who are struggling. The reach of God pressing out through those who shine with His light. Moral. Intense. Firm. Durable. The strong are fortified by the love which they spread generously, without judgment or censorship, to as many souls as they can.

The Joyful

A boy who remembered joy in a world of agony, living as an example of faith and hope when it seemed both should be lost to him; he glorified his Lord's love. He stood firm in his beliefs and strong in his faith even when his body broke down too far for him to stand on his own two feet. He believed and never wavered. He lives on in eternity with no pain to shadow his endless joy.

Joy is the result—the reward—of having the faith needed to relinquish your pain and sorrows to the Lord so that He can heal them. It is an all-encompassing feeling of love shining from deep within. Delight. Enjoyment. Fruition. Rapture. Visible to even those who do not know the Lord, it is contentment deep in the very being of a soul—a shining light inseparable from those who have learned to turn to God's love. It is the ability to smile in the harshest situations and be comforted in the darkest moments. Joy is the greatest example of God's love, as it is spread contagiously from one soul to the next.

The Loved

A child who carried life to an innocent. In the hands of the most unlikely hero, the Lord delivered a miracle. Hurt beyond words and abandoned to the harsh world herself, the still untouchable faith of a child let her save two souls in a hospital—and so many more she will never know. God smiles on His young daughter bright as the sun. His love for her is untouchable. His love is untouchable.

Love is indescribable and undefinable in its essence and the love of God is love in its purest form. It is not something you can understand or truly offer to another until you have felt it for yourself. It is the feeling which animates a person in all that they do—in all that they believe. That drives them to care for others. That creates the mercy of humanity. Healing. Life-giving. Devotion. Faith. Hope. It is the greatest of the gifts God has given to His children. The power that makes all else possible. God is love.

The Peaceful

A storm-tamer who wreaks havoc to deliver peace to those in pain. Faith as strong as rolling thunder and as devastating as a crack of lightening—she doesn't bend to any who would question her Lord. Willing to stand for her faith under the most daunting of circumstances, she is given the gift of washing the pain from others. The Lord kept her from fearing the storm and He rewarded her loyalty and faith by letting her become the storm that spreads fearlessness to lost souls.

Peace is the freedom not to have to fear. It is a miraculous gift built of faith, hope, and love—a gift from the Lord to His most loyal children. The accord of a soul and a heart that need not worry because they are safe in the hand of the Lord, working in harmony to spread His glory in the world. Peace is the lack of anxiety, the abundance of mercy. The absence of struggle, the assurance of love. Steady. Constant. Harmony. Serenity. Peace is accepting the unknown and knowing that the Lord's will, will prevail.

CPSIA information can be obtained
at www.ICGtesting.com
Printed in the USA
LVHW051621280121
677756LV00017B/1855